Battles in the Desert

40TH-ANNIVERSARY EDITION

José Emilio Pacheco

Battles in the Desert

*translated from the Spanish
by Katherine Silver*

*with an afterword
by Fernanda Melchor,
translated by Sophie Hughes*

A NEW DIRECTIONS PAPERBOOK

Originally published as *Las batallas en el desierto*
by Ediciones Era, S.A., Mexico City.

First published as New Directions Paperbook 1503 in 2021
Manufactured in the United States of America
Design by Erik Rieselbach

Library of Congress Cataloging-in-Publication Data
Names: Pacheco, José Emilio, author. | Silver, Katherine, translator. |
Melchor, Fernanda, 1982– writer of afterword.
Title: Battles in the desert / José Emilio Pacheco ; translated from
the Spanish by Katherine Silver ; with an afterword by Fernanda Melchor.
Other titles: Batallas en el desierto. English
Description: New York : New Directions Publishing Corporation, 2021. |
Originally published as Las batallas en el desierto
by Ediciones Era, S.A., Mexico City.
Identifiers: LCCN 2021001794 | ISBN 9780811230957 (paperback) |
ISBN 9780811230964 (ebook)
Classification: LCC PQ7298.26.A25 B3813 2021 | DDC 863/.64—dc23
LC record available at https://lccn.loc.gov/2021001794

2 4 6 8 10 9 7 5 3

New Directions Books are published for James Laughlin
by New Directions Publishing Corporation
80 Eighth Avenue, New York 10011

To the memory of José Estrada, Alberto Isaac,
and Juan Manuel Torres,

and to Eduardo Mejía

The past is a foreign country:
they do things differently there.

—L. P. Hartley, *The Go-Between*

Contents

1. *The Ancient World*

I remember—I don't remember: what year was that? There were already supermarkets but not television, only radio: *Las aventuras de Carlos Lacroix, Tarzan, The Lone Ranger, La Legión de los Madrugadores, Los Niños Catedráticos, Leyendas de la calles de México, Panseco, Dr. I.Q., Dr. Lovesick From Her Soul Hospital.* Paco Malgesto presented the bullfights, Carlos Albert wrote about soccer, and Pedro "El Mago" Septién was the baseball announcer. The first postwar cars were rolling through the streets: Packards, Cadillacs, Buicks, Chryslers, Mercurys, Hudsons, Pontiacs, Dodges, Plymouths, DeSotos. We went to see movies with Errol Flynn and Tyrone Power, to matinees that showed whole serials—*The Invasion of Mongo* was my favorite. The most popular songs were "Sin ti," "La rondalla," "La burrita," "La Múcura," "Amorcito Corazón." Once again, that classic Puerto Rican bolero, "Obsesíon," was playing everywhere:

9

However high the heavens or the skies,
however deep the ocean lies,
nothing in the world from you will keep,
my love for you so true and deep.

It was the year of polio: schools full of children wearing orthopedic devices; of foot-and-mouth disease: all over the country tens of thousands of sick livestock were being shot; of floods: the city center had turned back into a lake, people went drifting through the streets in boats. They say that the next storm will bust the sewage system, and the capital will be inundated. Who cares, my brother would say, under Miguel Alemán's regime we're up to our ears in shit anyway.

Everywhere the face of El Señorpresidente: huge murals, idealized portraits, ubiquitous photos, allegories of progress depicting Miguel Alemán as The Lord Our Father, fawning caricatures, monuments. Public adulation, incessant private abuse. We wrote in our punishment notebooks thousands of times: I must obey, I must obey, I must obey my parents and my teachers. They taught us the history of the fatherland, the national language, the geography of Mexico City—the rivers (there were still rivers), the mountains (the mountains could still be seen). It was the ancient world. The adults complained about inflation, changes, traffic, immorality, noise, crime, overpopulation, beggars, foreigners, corruption, the limitless wealth of the few and the abject misery of almost everyone else.

The newspapers stated: This is a harrowing time for the entire world. The specter of the war to end all wars hovers over the horizon; the mushroom cloud is the dismal symbol of our era. There was, however, hope. Our textbooks confirmed: As can be seen from the map, Mexico is shaped like a cornucopia, the horn of plenty. Universal well-being and abundance were predicted for the unimaginable year 2000, without any specifics about how we were going to achieve this. Sparkling clean cities free of injustice, poor people, violence, congestion, and garbage. Every family would have an ultramodern and aerodynamic house (words of the era). Nobody would want for anything; machines would do all the work. Streets full of trees and fountains, traversed by silent, smog-free vehicles that would never collide. Paradise on earth. Utopia finally achieved. In the meantime, we modernized, incorporating into our speech terms that had at first sounded like the pochismos from the Tin Tan movies, and then imperceptibly became Mexicanized: tancue, okai, wasamara, sherap, sarry, wan momen pleez. We began to eat hamburgesas, pyze, donas, jotdogs, malteadas, ayescreem, margarina, pinutbuter.

Coca-Cola was burying our aguas frescas made from hibiscus, chia seeds, and lime. The poor still drank tepache. Our parents soon got used to drinking haibols, which at first tasted to them like medicine. Tequila is forbidden in my house, I once heard my Uncle Julián say. I serve only whisky to my guests. We must whiten the taste of the Mexicans.

11. *The Ravages of War*

During recess we ate those tortas de nata that will never be seen again. When we played, we divided ourselves into two camps: Arabs and Jews. Israel had just been established, and there was a war against the Arab League. The kids who really were Jews and Arabs only ever called each other names or fought. Our teacher, Bernardo Mondragón, would say to them: You were born here. You are as Mexican as your fellow students. Don't pass on the hatred. After everything that has happened (the endless massacres, the extermination camps, the atomic bomb, the millions and millions dead), the world of tomorrow, the world you will become men in, should be a place of peace, free of crime and free of evil. A giggle rang out from the back row. Mondragón looked at us with great sadness, wondering what would become of us over the years, how many evils and how many catastrophes awaited us.

The Ottoman Empire lingered like the light of

a long-dead star. For me, a child of Colonia Roma, both Jews and Arabs were Turcos. But Turcos didn't seem as strange to me as Jim, who'd been born in San Francisco and spoke both languages with no accent; or Toru, who grew up in a concentration camp for the Japanese; or Peralta and Rosales, who didn't pay tuition, had scholarships, and lived in the dilapidated parts of Colonia Doctores. La Calzada de la Piedad, still not renamed Avenida Cuauhtémoc, and Parque Jesús Urueta formed the dividing line between the colonias Roma and Doctores. Colonia Romita was another town altogether. There lurks the Sack Man, the great Childrobber. If you go to Romita, my boy, they will kidnap you, gouge out your eyes, cut off your hands and your tongue, send you out to beg for alms, and the Sack Man will take everything. By day he is a beggar, by night an elegant millionaire, enriched by exploiting his victims. The fear of getting too close to Romita. The fear of riding the streetcar over the bridge on Avenida Coyoacán—only rails and girders, and the dirty Río La Piedad, which sometimes overflows when it rains, below.

Before the war in the Middle East, our class's main sport was harassing Toru. Chinaman, Chinaman, Japanese: eat your shit on your knees. Hey Toru, Toro: try charging us and we'll stab you with banderillas. I never joined in on the taunts. I thought about how I'd feel as the only Mexican boy in a school in Tokyo, and how Toru must feel when he sees those movies where the Japanese are portrayed as jibbering apes and die by the millions. Toru, the best student in class, outstanding in every subject. Always studying, book in hand. He knew jujitsu. One day he'd had enough and nearly ripped Domínguez to shreds. He forced him to get down on his knees and beg for forgiveness. Nobody messed with Toru again. Today he manages a Japanese factory with four thousand Mexican slaves.

I'm in the Irgun. I'll kill you: I'm in the Arab Legion. The battles in the desert began. We called it a desert because it was a reddish yard of brick and volcanic rock, without a single plant or tree, only a cement box at the back. This concealed the entry to an underground passageway, built during the times of religious persecution to reach the house on the corner, and from there to flee down the other street. We thought of this underground tunnel as a vestige of a prehistoric era. At that moment, however, the Cristero War was less remote from us than our childhood is from us now. A war my mother's family participated in as more than mere sympathizers. Twenty years later they were still worshipping martyrs like Father Pro and Anacleto González Flores. On the other hand, nobody remembered the thousands of dead peasants, the agrarian reformers, the rural teachers, the press-gangs.

I didn't understand anything. For me, war, any war, was the stuff of movies. Sooner or later the good guys win (who are the good guys?). In Mexico, fortunately, there'd been no war since General Cárdenas defeated the Saturnino Cedillo uprising. My parents found this difficult to believe, however, because their childhood, adolescence, and youth had been spent against a backdrop of constant battles and executions. But that year, or so it seemed, things were going quite well; they were always cancelling class so they could take us to inauguration ceremonies for highways, avenues, dams, sports complexes, hospitals, ministries, enormous buildings.

As a rule, there was nothing but a pile of rocks. The president dedicated huge unfinished monuments to himself. Hours and hours under the sun without moving or drinking water—Rosales brought lemons, they're good to quench your thirst, pass one over here—awaiting the arrival of Miguel Alemán— young, smiling, warmhearted, dazzling, waving from a flatbed truck, surrounded by his retinue.

Applause, confetti, paper streamers, flowers, young women, soldiers (still wearing their French helmets), gunslingers (nobody yet called them bodyguards), the perennial little old lady who breaks through the line of soldiers and is photographed as she hands El Señorpresidente a bouquet of roses.

I'd had several friend, but my parents didn't like any of them: Jorge, because he was the son of a general who fought against the Cristeros; Arturo, because his parents were divorced and he was looked after by an aunt who made money reading people's fortunes; Alberto, because his widowed mother worked at a travel agency, and no decent woman ever worked outside the home. That year I made friends with Jim. During those ceremonies, which had become a normal part of life, Jim would say: Today my father's coming. And then: See him? He's the one with the navy-blue tie—there he is, next to President Alemán. But nobody could pick his father out among all the other little heads plastered with linseed oil or Glostura. But his picture often appeared in the papers and Jim carried the clippings around in his knapsack. Did you see my father in *El Excélsior?* How weird, you don't look anything like him. They say I take after my mother. I'm going to look like him when I grow up.

III. *Ali Baba and the Forty Thieves*

How was it that Jim's father held such an important position in the government, wielding so much influence over the business world, yet Jim was attending a second-rate school, a school befitting the likes of us denizens of the very downwardly mobile Colonia Roma, hardly the spot for the son of Miguel Alemán's superpowerful bosom buddy and banking partner, a man who earned millions every time the president sneezed: on contracts here, there, and everywhere; on land deals in Acapulco; import and construction permits; on authorizations to set up subsidiaries of North American companies; on laws requiring the installation of water tanks lined with carcinogenic asbestos on every rooftop; on the resale of powered milk stolen from free school breakfast programs in the poorest neighborhood; the counterfeiting of vaccines and medicines; on huge gold and silver smuggling rings; on large tracts of land bought for centavos per meter weeks before the announcement of a new road or development project that would increase their value ten-thousandfold; or on hundreds of millions of pesos changed to dollars and deposited in Switzerland the day before a devaluation.

What turned out to be even more unfathomable was that Jim lived with his mother in a third-floor apartment near school—not in a house in Las Lomas, or at least in Polanco. How strange. Not really, they'd say during recess. Jim's mother is that guy's *mistress.* His wife is that horrible old bag who always appears in the newspaper society pages. Whenever there's an event for poor children (haha, my father says that first they make them poor and then they give them charity), she's there—ugly, obese—getting photographed. They say she looks like a combination of a macaw and a mammoth. Jim's mother, on the other hand, is very young and very beautiful—some people even think she's his sister. And, Ayala chimed in, Jim's father is not that son-of-a-bitch thief fucking over Mexico—he's the son of a gringo journalist who took his mother to San Francisco and never married her. The Señor isn't very nice to poor Jim. They say he's got women all over the place—movie stars and stuff like that. Jim's mother is just one among many.

That's not true, I'd snap back. Don't be so mean. How would you like it if they talked about your mothers that way? Nobody dared say these things directly to Jim, but, as if intuiting the gossip, he'd explain: I don't see my father very much because he's always away, serving his country. Yeah, sure thing, Alcaraz would say, "serving his country"—Ali Baba and his forty thieves. At my house they say they're even stealing what's not there to steal. The entire Alemán government is a den of thieves. Maybe they'll buy you a new sweater with the money they steal from the rest of us.

Jim gets into quarrels and refuses to talk to anybody. I can only imagine what he'd do if he heard some of the things they say about his mother. (When he's around, our classmates limit their attacks to the Señor.) Jim has become my friend because I don't judge him. In a nutshell, it's not his fault. Nobody chooses how they're born, where they're born, when they're born, or to whom they're born. And we decided not to take part in the recess wars anymore—today the Jews took over Jerusalem, but tomorrow the Arabs will wreak their revenge.

Fridays after school I'd go with Jim to La Roma, El Royal, El Balmori, movie houses that no longer exist, to see movies with Lassie or the teenage Elizabeth Taylor. Our favorite was a triple feature we saw a thousand times: *Frankenstein*, *Dracula*, and *The Wolf Man*. Or a double feature—*Objective: Burma* and *God*

Is My Co-Pilot. Or maybe the one Father Pérez del Valle loved to show on Sundays at his Club Vanguardias: *Goodbye, Mr. Chips*. That was as sad as *Bambi*. I saw that Walt Disney movie when I was three or four years old, and they had to drag me out of the theater sobbing because the hunters killed Bambi's mother. During the war they murdered millions of mothers, but I didn't know that, and I wasn't crying for them or their children, even though in Cinelandia—along with the Donald Duck, Mickey Mouse, Popeye the Sailor Man, Woody Woodpecker, and Bugs Bunny cartoons—they showed newsreels: bombs flattening cities, cannons, battles, fires, rubble, dead bodies.

IV. *A Place In Between*

I had so many brothers and sisters living at home
that I couldn't invite Jim over. My mother was always picking up after us, cooking, washing clothes,
eager to buy a washing machine, vacuum cleaner,
blender, pressure cooker, electric refrigerator (our
fridge was one of the last that required a fresh block
of ice every morning). At that time my mother could
see only the narrow horizon she'd been shown while
growing up. She despised anyone who wasn't from
Jalisco. She considered all other Mexicans foreigners and particularly loathed those from the capital.
She hated Colonia Roma because all the good families were starting to leave, and there were more and
more Arabs and Jews and people from the south—
Campeche, Chiapas, Tabasco, the Yucatán. She be-
rated Héctor, who was twenty years old and, instead
of attending his classes at the National University,
spent his days at the Swing Club and in pool halls,
cantinas, and bordellos. My brother's passion was

talking about women, politics, and automobiles. All that complaining about the military, he'd say, and now you see what happens when they put a civilian in as president. With General Henríquez Guzmán, Mexico would be as great as Argentina under General Perón. They'll see, they'll see what'll happen in 1952. I'll lay odds that Henríquez Guzmán will be president, with or without the PRI.

My father spent all his time at his soap factory, which was being drowned by the competition: North American brands and their marketing campaigns. They advertised the new detergents—Ace, Fab, Vel—on the radio, proclaiming that soap was a thing of the past. Those new suds that meant cleanliness, comfort, and well-being for everybody else (still ignorant of the dangers)—and for women meant liberation from endless hours at the washbasin—was for our family the foamy crest of the wave washing away our privileges.

Monsignor Martínez, the archbishop of Mexico, decreed one day of prayer and penance to halt the spread of communism. I'll never forget one morning during recess, I was showing Jim one of my Big Little Books, illustrated novels that had on the upper edge of the pages a flipbook—the figures moved if you flipped quickly through them with your thumb. Rosales, who'd never picked on me before, shouted:

Hey, look at those two faggots. Let's give those faggots noogies. I started punching him: Let's start talking about your mother, you sonofabitch, and then we'll see who's a faggot, you stupid indio. The teacher pulled us apart. I had a split lip, and his nose was bleeding all over his shirt.

Thanks to that fight, my father taught me not to denigrate others. He asked who I'd fought with. I called Rosales an indio. My father said that in Mexico we are all Indians even if we don't know it or want to admit it. If the Indians weren't poor, nobody would use that word as an insult. I called Rosales pelado, slum scum. My father pointed out to me that it's not their fault they're poor, and before judging anyone else I should ask myself if he's had the same opportunities as me.

I was a millionaire compared to Rosales; compared to Harry Atherton, I was a beggar. The previous year, while I was still attending Colegio México, Harry Atherton invited me over to his house in Las Lomas—underground billiards room, swimming pool, a library with thousands of leather-bound volumes, storehouse, wine cellar, gymnasium, steam bath, tennis courts, six bathrooms. (Why do the homes of rich Mexicans have so many bathrooms?) His bedroom looked out over a gently sloping garden with ancient trees and an artificial waterfall. Harry had been sent to Colegio México rather than the American School so he could become familiar with a Spanish-speaking milieu and from an early age get to know those who would be his assistants, his front men, his eternal apprentices, his servants.

We ate dinner. His parents didn't say a word to me and spoke English the whole time. Honey, how do you like the little Spic? He's a midget, isn't he? Oh, Jack, please. Maybe the poor kid is catching on. Don't worry, dear, he doesn't understand a thing. The next day, Harry said to me: I'm going to give you some advice. Learn how to use your cutlery, last night you ate your steak with your fish fork. And don't make so much noise with your soup, don't talk with your mouth full, chew slowly, and take small bites.

The opposite happened with Rosales right after I started this school, when the crisis at my father's factory made it impossible for him to pay the Colegio México tuition. I went to Rosales's house to copy his Civics notes. He was an excellent student, one of the best in composition and spelling, and we all relied on him for these favors. He lived in a neighborhood built out of scrap lumber. The broken pipes flooded the yard. Shit bobbed around in the greenish water.

At twenty-seven his mother looked fifty. She welcomed me warmly, and even though I hadn't been invited, she insisted I join them for dinner. Brain quesadillas. They were disgusting. A really strange grease, like car oil, oozed out of them. Rosales slept on a petate in the living room. His mother's new boyfriend had kicked him out of the only bedroom.

v. *However Deep the Ocean Lies*

My fight with Rosales convinced Jim that I was his
friend. One Friday, he did something he had never
done before: he invited me to his house after school
for supper. Too bad I couldn't invite him to mine.
We walked up to the third floor, and he opened the
door. I have a key because my mother doesn't like
to have a maid. Tidy and very clean, the apartment
smelled of perfume. Brand-new furniture from Sears
Roebuck. A photograph of his mother by Semo, one
of Jim on his first birthday (the Golden Gate Bridge
in the background), several of the Señor with the
president at ceremonies, inaugurations, on the presidential Tren Olivo train car, on the presidential El
Mexicano airplane, and in group photos. "The Cub
of the Revolution," as the president was called, and
his team. The first university graduates to govern the
country. Technocrats, not politicians. Impeccable
moral character, according to the propaganda.

I never imagined Jim's mother would be so young,

so elegant, and above all, so beautiful. I didn't know what to say to her. I can't describe how I felt when she shook my hand. I would have liked to just stand there, staring at her. Please go on into Jim's room. I'll finish preparing your supper. Jim showed me his collection of ballpoint pens (fountain pens smelled nasty and leaked slimy ink; ballpoints were all the rage that year when we used ink wells, pen holders, and blotters for the last time), and the toys the Señor bought in the United States—a cannon that shot caps, jet fighter planes, soldiers with flamethrowers, windup tanks, plastic machine guns (it was the beginning of plastics), a Lionel electric train set, a portable radio. I don't bring any of these to school because nobody in Mexico has toys like these. No, of course not. As children of the Second World War, we didn't have toys. Everything had gone into military production. I read in *Reader's Digest* that even Parker and Esterbrook manufactured war materiel instead of pens. But I couldn't have cared less about the toys. Hey, what did you say your mother's name was? Mariana. That's what I call her. I don't call her Mamá. What about you? No, I mean, I even address my mother formally, she does the same with my grandparents. Don't make fun of me, Jim, don't laugh at me.

Come to eat, Mariana said. And we sat down. I sat

across from her, staring at her. I didn't know what to do: not eat a bite or devour everything to flatter her. If I eat, she'll think I'm starving; if I don't eat, she'll think I don't like what she made. Chew slowly, don't talk with your mouth full. What can we talk about? Luckily Mariana breaks the silence. What do you think of these sandwiches grilled on this appliance? They're called flying saucers, platos voladores. I love them, Señora, I've never tasted anything so delicious. Pan Bimbo—sliced white bread—ham, Kraft cheese, bacon, butter, ketchup, mayonnaise, mustard: the exact opposite of the pozole, birria, tostada de pata, and chicharrón with salsa verde that my mother made. Do you want more platos voladores? I'd be happy to make more for you. No, thank you, Señora. They're scrumptious, but really, please don't bother.

She didn't touch a thing. She talked, talked to me the whole time. Jim was silent, eating one flying saucer after another. Mariana asked me: What does your father do? I was so embarrassed to say he owns a factory that makes bath and laundry soap. The new detergents are putting him out of business. Oh, really? I'd never thought about that. Pause, silence. How many brothers and sisters do you have? Three sisters and one brother. Were you all born here, in Mexico City? Only me and my youngest sister, the rest were born in Guadalajara. We used to have a very big house on Calle San Francisco. It's been torn down. Do you like school? School's not bad, right, Jim? Though our classmates are pretty annoying.

Well, Señora, if you will please excuse me, I have to go. (How to explain to her that they'll kill me if I get home after eight?) Thanks a lot, Señora. Everything was really delicious. I'm going to tell my mother to buy one of those grills and make me flying saucers. There aren't any in Mexico, Jim interjected for the first time. If you want, I'll bring one back for you from the States when I go.

You are always welcome here. Come back soon. Thanks again, Señora. Thanks, Jim. See you Monday. How I would have loved to remain there forever or at least take with me the photograph of Mariana in the living room. I walked down Avenida Tabasco, then turned onto Córdoba to get to my house on Zacatecas. The mercury streetlamps emitted a dim light. City in shadows, mysterious Colonia Roma of those days. One atom of a big wide world, prepared many years before my birth, as if staged for my performance. A jukebox played a bolero. Until that moment, music had been only the national anthem, church hymns, Cri-Cri's children's songs—"Los caballitos," "Marcha de las letras," "Negrito sandía," "El ratón vaquero," "Juan Pestañas"—and that circular, dense, absorbing melody by Ravel that XEQ played at the beginning of its broadcasts at six thirty in the morning, when my father turned on the radio to wake me up to the clamor of *La Legión de los Madrugadores*. When I heard the other bolero that had nothing to do with Ravel's, the words caught my attention:

> *However high the heavens or the skies,*
> *however deep the ocean lies.*

I looked down Avenida Álvaro Obregón and said to myself: I'm going to hold onto my memory of this moment because everything that now exists will never be the same again. One day I'll view all this as the most remote prehistory. I'm going to preserve it all intact because today I fell in love with Mariana. What's going to happen? Nothing will happen. Nothing could possibly happen. What will I do? Change schools so I don't see Jim and therefore don't see Mariana? Look for a girl my own age? But at my age nobody can *look* for a girl. The only thing anybody can do is fall in love secretly, silently, like I have with Mariana. Fall in love knowing that all is lost and there is no hope.

VI. *Obsession*

You're very late. Mamá, I told you I was going to Jim's house after school. That might be, but nobody gave you permission to come home at this time of night—it's eight thirty. I was so worried; I thought you'd been killed or kidnapped by the Sack Man. What garbage have you been eating? It's anybody's guess who your *little friend's* parents are. Is he the one you go to the movies with?

Yes, he is. His father is very important. He's in the government. In the government? And he lives in that grubby building? Why didn't you tell me that before? What did you say his name was? Impossible, I know his wife. She and Aunt Elena are good friends. They don't have any children. It's a tragedy in the midst of so much wealth and power. They're pulling the wool over your eyes, Carlitos. I don't know why, but they're pulling the wool over your eyes. I'm going to ask your teacher to sort out this mystery. No, please, I beg you, don't say anything to Mondragón.

What would Jim's mother think if she found out? She was so nice to me. Oh, no, that's all I need! What are you hiding? Tell me the truth. You didn't really go to this so-called Jim's house?

I finally convinced my mother. Even so, she still suspected that something untoward had taken place. I spent a very sad weekend. I became a child again and went to Plaza Ajusco to play alone with my little wooden cars. Plaza Ajusco, where they would take me to sunbathe when I was a newborn and where I learned to walk. Some of the surrounding houses, built during the time of Porfirio Díaz, had already been demolished to make room for ugly new buildings. The figure-eight fountain, full of dead insects floating on the surface of the water. And between my house and the park lived Doña Sara P. de Madero. I thought it was incredible to see in person, even if from afar, someone who is written about in history books, someone who played a role in events that occurred forty years before. That fragile, dignified old woman, still in mourning for her assassinated husband.

I was playing in Plaza Ajusco, and one part of me reasoned: How can you have fallen in love with Mariana after seeing her only once, and she's old enough to be your mother? It's idiotic and ridiculous—there's no way she'll love you in return. But another part, the strongest part, was deaf to all reasoning. I kept repeating her name as if uttering it would bring her closer to me. Monday was worse. Jim said: Mariana really liked you. She's glad we're friends. I thought: she noticed me, she paid attention to me, she realized—a little, at least a little—how strong an impression she'd made on me.

For weeks and weeks I'd ask Jim about her, using any pretext I could think of so he wouldn't think it strange. I tried to disguise my interest and at the same time get him to tell me more about Mariana. Jim never told me something I didn't already know. Apparently he didn't know anything about his own past. I can't imagine how everybody else could have known. I begged him again and again to let me come to his house to see his toys, his illustrated books, his comics. Jim read comics in English that Mariana bought for him at Sanborns. He looked down his nose at ours: *Pepín*, *Paquín*, *Chamaco*, *Carones*; for the privileged few: the Argentinean *Billiken* or the Chilean *Peneca*.

Since they always gave us a lot of homework, I could go over to Jim's house only on Fridays. That was when Mariana was at the beauty salon getting ready for her night out with the Señor. She always returned around eight thirty or nine, and I could never stay till then to see her. Our supper was always ready for us in the refrigerator: chicken salad, cole-slaw, cold cuts, apple pie. Once, when Jim opened a closet, out fell a picture of Mariana at six months old, lying naked on a tiger-skin rug. I felt an enormous wave of tenderness when I realized something that nobody ever thinks about because it's too obvious: Mariana was also a little girl, was also my age, will also be a woman like my mother, and then an old lady like my grandmother. But at that moment she was the most beautiful woman in the world, and I thought about her every second of every day. Mariana had become my obsession.

However high the heavens and the skies,
however deep the ocean lies.

VII. *Today More Than Ever*

Until one day—one of those cloudy days I love and nobody else likes—I couldn't stand it any longer. We were in national language class, as they used to call Spanish. Mondragón was teaching us the pluperfect subjunctive, "would have loved": hubiera or hubiese amado, hubiéramos or hubiésemos amado, hubierais or hubieseis amado, hubieran or hubiesan amado. It was eleven o'clock. I asked permission to go to the bathroom. Then I sneaked out of school. I rang the doorbell to apartment four. One, two, three times. Mariana finally came to the door—fresh, beautiful, without makeup. She was wearing a silk kimono. She was holding a razor just like my father's but in miniature. When I rang the bell she'd been shaving her legs or her underarms. She was, of course, surprised to see me. Carlos, what are you doing here? Did something happen to Jim? No, Señora. Jim is fine, nothing's wrong.

We sat down on the couch. Mariana crossed

her legs. For a second the kimono opened ever so slightly. Her knees, her thighs, her breasts, her flat belly, her mysterious hidden sex. Nothing's wrong, I repeated. It's just that ... I don't know how to say this, Señora. I'm so embarrassed. What are you going to think of me? Carlos, I really don't understand. It's very strange to see you here like this at this time of day. You should be at school, shouldn't you? Yes, of course, it's just that I can't stand it any longer. I sneaked out, left without permission. If they find out, they'll expel me. Nobody knows I'm with you. Please, don't tell anybody I came here. Don't tell Jim. I beg you, least of all Jim. Promise me you won't.

But, why are you so worked up? Did something terrible happen at home? Are you in trouble at school? Do you want some chocolate milk, Coca-Cola, a glass of soda water? You can trust me. Tell me how I can help you. No, Señora, you can't help me. Why not, Carlitos? Because what I came here to tell you—once and for all, Señora, and please forgive me—is that I'm in love with you.

I thought she was going to laugh, shout at me: You're crazy. Or maybe: Get out of here, I'm going to tell your parents and your teacher. I dreaded all of these, the normal reactions. But Mariana was neither outraged nor scornful. She looked at me sadly.

She took my hand (I'll never forget that she took my hand) and she said:

I understand you, you have no idea how well. Now you have to understand me and face the fact that you are a child like my son and for you I am an old lady—I just turned twenty-eight. So not now and not ever could there be anything between us. You understand me, don't you? I don't want you to suffer. Many terrible things await you, poor boy. Think of this as something amusing, Carlos, something that you'll be able to remember with a smile when you grow up, not with hard feelings. Come back here with Jim and keep treating me as what I am: your best friend's mother. Keep coming over here with Jim, act like nothing's happened, and that's how this *infatuation*—forgive me, falling in love—will pass, will avoid becoming a problem for you, a tragedy that could damage your whole life.

I felt like crying. I controlled myself and said: You're right, Señora. I understand everything. I'm so grateful to you for what you said. Forgive me. No matter what, I had to tell you. I was going to die if I didn't tell you. I have nothing to forgive you for, Carlos. I like that you're honest and that you deal with your feelings. Please don't tell Jim. I won't tell him, don't worry.

I freed my hand from hers. I got up to leave. Then Mariana stopped me: Before you leave, can I ask you a favor? Let me give you a kiss. And she gave me a kiss, a quick kiss, not exactly on the lips, closer to the corner of my mouth. A kiss just like the ones Jim got before leaving for school. I shuddered. I didn't kiss her back. I didn't say anything. I ran down the stairs. Instead of returning to school, I walked to Insurgentes. I arrived home in a state of total confusion. I claimed that I was sick and wanted to go lie down.

But the teacher had just called. Alarmed when I didn't come back to class, they looked for me in the bathrooms, all over school, and Jim had said: He must have gone to visit my mother. At this time of day? Yeah. Carlitos is a weirdo. You never know what's up with him. I think he's got a screw loose. He's got a brother who's a half-crazed hoodlum.

Mondragón and Jim went to the apartment. Mariana confessed that I'd been there for a few minutes because the Friday before I'd left my history book there. This lie made Jim furious. I don't know how, but he understood everything and explained it to the teacher. Mondragón called the factory and the house to tell them what I'd done, even though Mariana denied it. Her denial made me even more suspect in the eyes of Jim, Mondragón, and my parents.

VIII. *The Prince of This World*

I never thought of you as a freak. Where have you seen such bad role models? Tell me the truth, was it Héctor who put you up to this? Anybody who corrupts a child deserves a slow, painful death and all of hell's punishments. Come on, speak up, don't just sit there crying like a little sissy. Tell me it was your brother who led you astray.

But, Mamá, I don't think I did anything so wrong. And you still have the gall to claim you've done nothing wrong? As soon as your fever drops, you're going to confess and take communion so that Our Lord Jesus Christ can forgive you your sins. My father didn't yell at me at all. He simply said: This boy isn't normal. There's something not working right upstairs. It must be from when he fell on his head at six months old in Plaza Ajusco. I'm going to take him to see a specialist.

We're all hypocrites, unable to see ourselves or judge ourselves as we see and judge others. Even I,

43

who never knew anything about anything, realized that for years my father had been supporting a second family—his ex-secretary and the two children he'd had with her. I remembered what had happened once at the barbershop while I was waiting to get my hair cut. Some copies of *Vea* and *Vodevil* were lying next to the news magazines. I waited until the barber and his customer were distracted, saying bad things about the government. I hid the *Vea* inside the *Hoy* and looked at the pictures of Tongolele, Su Muy Key, Kalantán, almost naked. Legs, breasts, mouth, waist, hips, the mysterious hidden sex.

The barber—who shaved my father every day and had been cutting my hair since I turned one—saw the look on my face in the mirror. Put that down, Carlitos. Those are for grownups. I'm going to tell your father on you. Which meant, I thought, that if you're a child you have no right to like women. And if you don't accept that edict, they make a great big fuss and say you're crazy. So unfair.

When, I wondered, was the first time I became aware of desire? Maybe a year earlier in the Cine Chapultepec, when I saw Jennifer Jones's naked shoulder in *Duel in the Sun*. Or maybe when I saw Antonia's legs when she'd hitch up her skirt to mop the floor painted Congo yellow. Antonia was very pretty, and she was nice to me. Even so, I would say to her:

You're bad because you kill chickens. It horrified me to watch them die—better to buy them already dead and plucked, but that was only just beginning to be the custom. Antonia left because Héctor wouldn't leave her alone.

I didn't return to school, and they didn't let me to go out anywhere. We went to Nuestra Señora del Rosario church, where we heard Mass on Sundays, and where I'd had my First Holy Communion, and, where, thanks to my First Fridays devotions, I was still accumulating indulgences. My mother sat in one of the pews and prayed for my soul, in danger of eternal damnation. I knelt in front of the confessional. Dying of embarrassment, I told Father Ferrán everything.

In a low and slightly panting voice, Father Ferrán asked me for details: Was she naked? Was there a man in the house? Do you think she'd committed a shameful act before opening the door? And then: Have you ever abused yourself? Have you caused your seed to spill? I don't know what that is, Father. He gave me a very detailed explanation. Then he regretted his words, realizing that he was talking to a child who was as yet incapable of producing the raw material to spill anything, and launched off on a speech I didn't understand: Because of original sin, the devil is the prince of this world, and he sets traps for us, giving us ample opportunities to stray from the love of God and leading us into sin—one more thorn in the crown of Our Lord Jesus Christ.

I said: Yes, Father. Though somehow I couldn't imagine the devil personally bothering to lead me into temptation. Much less Christ suffering because I'd fallen in love with Mariana. As is de rigueur, I showed a willingness to mend my ways. But I wasn't repentant and I didn't feel guilty. Loving someone is not a sin, love is good, and the only demonic thing is hatred. That afternoon, Father Ferrán's moral exhortations impressed me less than the practical guide to masturbation he unwittingly provided. I arrived home eager to abuse myself and cause my seed to spill. I didn't do it. I recited twenty Our Fathers and fifty Hail Marys. I took communion the following day. In the evening, they took me to a psychiatrist's office with white walls and chrome furniture.

IX. *Mandatory English*

The psychiatrist asked me questions and wrote down everything I said on yellow lined paper. I didn't know how to answer. I didn't know the vocabulary of his profession, so no communication was possible. I had never imagined the things he asked me about my mother and my sisters. Then they made me draw every member of my family and trees and houses. Afterward they gave me the Rorschach test (is there anyone who doesn't see monsters in those ink blots?), and tests with numbers and geometric figures, and sentences I had to complete. They were as dumb as my answers:

My favorite thing is to climb trees and scale the walls of old houses, lemon sherbet, rainy days, adventure movies, Salgari novels. On second thought: to stay in bed awake, but my father makes me get up at six thirty to do exercises, even on Saturdays and Sundays. *What I hate most* is cruelty to people and animals, violence, loud voices, boasting, older brothers

47

who are bullies, arithmetic, that some people have nothing to eat while others have everything, finding garlic cloves in rice or stew, that they prune trees or chop them down, seeing bread being thrown away.

The girl who administered the final tests and the man talked in front of me. They acted as if I were a piece of furniture. Doctor, it is clearly an Oedipal issue. The child's intelligence is well below average. He's been overprotected and is submissive. A castrating mother, perhaps a primal scene. He went to see that woman knowing that he might find her with her lover. I'm sorry, Elisita, but I am of the opposite opinion. The boy is highly intelligent and unusually precocious, so much so that by the time he turns fifteen, he may turn into a perfect idiot. His abnormal behavior stems from neglect, excessive demands from both parents, a strong inferiority complex. Don't forget, he's very short for his age, and he's the youngest male child. Notice how he identifies with the victims, with animals and trees that can't defend themselves. He is looking for the affection that he cannot find within the family constellation.

I felt like shouting at them: You idiots, at least come to an agreement before you blab on with your stupid nonsense in a language that you yourselves don't even understand. Why do you have to label everything? Why can't you admit that a person can simply fall in love? Haven't you ever fallen in love? But the man came over to me and said: You can go now, son. We'll send the test results to your father.

My father was sitting solemnly in the waiting room surrounded by beat-up issues of *Life*, *Look*, and *Holiday*, proud to be able to read them fluently. He had just passed, at the top of his class, an intensive adult night course in English, and every day he practiced with records and workbooks. How strange to see a person his age, an old man of forty-eight, studying. Very early in the morning, after his exercises and before breakfast, he reviewed irregular verbs: be, was/were, been; have, had, had; get, got, gotten; break, broke, broken; forget, forgot, forgotten—and pronunciation—apple, world, country, people, business—so effortless for Jim and so difficult for him.

Those were terrible weeks. Héctor was the only one who took my side: You outdid yourself, Carlitos. A major step forward, in my humble opinion. Going after a chick that hot at your tender age; she's even hotter than Rita Hayworth. Fucking Carlos, who knows what you'll do when you're all grown up. Good for you trying to catch some action now before you're really up for it, instead of just jerking off. What a relief that neither of us turned out queer with so many sisters. But watch your step, Carlitos.

If that asshole finds out, he'll set his goons on you and beat the shit out of you. But, Héctor, man, it's not such a big deal. All I did was tell her I was in love with her. What's wrong with that? I didn't do anything. Seriously, I don't understand all the fuss.

It was bound to happen, my mother insisted, what with your father being so miserly, never having any money for his children—even though he has plenty to throw away on *other* expenses—and you ending up at a school for lowlifes, you unfortunate child. Imagine, letting the son of a woman like that study there! We have to enroll you in a place where there are only people of our class. And Héctor: But, Mamá, which class is that? We're perfect wannabes, the typical has-been family of Colonia Roma, the essence of the Mexican middle class. Carlos is just fine there. His school is perfect for the likes of us. Where are you going to put him?

x. *Rain of Fire*

My mother always insisted that our family—that is, her family—was one of the best families of Guadalajara. Never had they seen such a scandal as mine. Honorable, hardworking men. Devout women, selfless wives, exemplary mothers. Obedient and respectful children. But then came the revenge of the Indian hordes and the rabble against decency and the well-born. The Revolution—that is, the old caciques—stole our land and our house on Calle San Francisco with the excuse that our family was full of Cristeros. On top of that, my father—looked down on as the son of a tailor despite his engineering degree—squandered the inheritance from his father-in-law on ridiculous business ventures such as an airline with flights between cities inside Mexico, and a company exporting tequila to the United States. Then, with money borrowed from my mother's brothers, he bought the soap factory, which did well enough during the war but was going under when North American companies invaded the local market.

That's why, my mother never tired of repeating, we were in this accursed Mexico City. This wicked place, Sodom and Gomorrah, awaiting the rain of fire; a hell full of horrors—things never seen in Guadalajara, like the crime I'd just committed. Sinister capital city where we were forced to mingle with the very worst sort of people. Contagion, bad role models. Judge a man by the company he keeps. How was it possible, she repeated, that a supposedly *decent* school would accept that bastard (what's a bastard?), that spawn of a lady of the night. Because there's really no way of knowing who the father might be, what with all her clients, that harlot, that corrupter of minors. (What does spawn mean? What's a lady of the night? Why do you call her a harlot?)

My mother had forgotten all about Héctor, Héctor who boasted about being a hired goon at the university. It was rumored that he was one of the right-wing militants who forced Zubirán, the rector, to resign, and that he'd painted over the words "Dios no existe" on Diego Rivera's mural in the Hotel del Prado. Héctor was reading *Mein Kampf*, books about Field Marshal Rommel, *A Brief History of Mexico* by Vasconcelos, The *Stallion in the Harem, Insatiable Nights, Memoirs of a Nymphomaniac*, pornographic novels published in Havana and sold under the counter on San Juan de Letrán and in the area around Tívoli. My father devoured *How to Win Friends and Influence People*, *Self Mastery Through Conscious Auto-suggestion*, *The Power of Positive Thinking*, *Life Begins at Forty*. While my mother did her housework, she listened to all the radio soap operas on XEW, and sometimes, to relax, she'd read something by Hugo Wast or M. Delly.

Ah, Héctor, to see him now, to see the lean, bald, solemn, elegant industrialist my brother has become. So much gravitas, so serious, so devout, so respectable, so dignified in his role as a businessman in service to the multinationals. A Catholic gentleman, the father of eleven children, a distinguished member of the Mexican extreme right (in this respect, at least, he's always been infallibly consistent).

But in those days, maids would flee "the young master," who'd try to rape them. Egged on by his gang's ditty, "Dip into your maid's honeypot: it's always free and always hot," Héctor would burst into their room on the rooftop at midnight, naked and erect, inflamed by the purple prose of his novels. He would tussle with the girls and as he attacked and they defended themselves, Héctor would ejaculate on their nightgowns, without managing to penetrate them. The shouts would wake up my parents. They'd go upstairs. My sisters and I would watch, huddled together, from the bottom of the spiral staircase. They'd yell at Héctor, threaten to throw him out of the house. Right then and there, in the middle of the night, they'd fire the maid, even more guilty than "the young master" for *provoking* him. Héctor got venereal diseases from the whores around Plaza Meave or 2 de Abril, and then in the feuds between rival gangs on the banks of Río de la Piedad Héctor got his teeth broken when a rock was thrown at him. Héctor smashed a locksmith's skull with a rubber pipe, and there was a trip to the police station because Héctor had taken drugs with his friends in Parque Urueta and ransacked a Chinese restaurant (my father had to pay a fine and damages and pull strings in the government so Héctor wouldn't go to prison). When I heard that Héctor had taken drugs, I thought he owed money, because in my house debts were always referred to as drugs. (In this respect, my father was the perfect drug addict.) Later, Isabel, my oldest sister, explained to me what had been going on. It was only natural for Héctor to take my side; for the moment, I'd replaced him as the black sheep of the family.

XI. *Specters*

There was more trouble at the beginning of the year when Isabel started going out with Esteban. In the thirties, Esteban had been a famous child actor. When he grew up, he lost his sweet voice and innocent face. He no longer got parts in movies or on stage, so he earned his living reading jokes on XEW, drank like a fish, and was determined to marry Isabel and go to Hollywood to try his luck even though he didn't speak a word of English. He would come drunk to see her, without a tie, stinking to high heaven, his suit stained and his shoes dirty.

Nobody understood why Isabel was such a devoted fan. She thought Esteban was splendid because she'd seen him during his golden age, and—in the absence of Tyrone Power, Errol Flynn, Clark Gable, Robert Mitchum, and Cary Grant—Esteban was Isabel's only chance to kiss a movie star, even if he only acted in Mexican movies, and he was a favorite butt of family jokes, almost as handy for derision as Miguel Alemán's regime. Have you ever noticed that Pedro Infante has the mug of a chauffeur? No wonder all the servant girls adore him.

One night, my father shouted at Esteban and shoved him, then threw him out of the house. Arriving home late from English class, he'd found Esteban in the living room with the lights low and his hand up Isabel's skirt. Outside, Héctor punched him, knocked him down, and then started kicking him until Esteban, covered in blood, managed to get to his feet and scurry off like a dog. Isabel refused to speak to Héctor and would attack me at the slightest provocation, even though I'd tried to stop my brother from kicking poor Esteban when he was down. Isabel and Esteban never saw each other again. A short time later, brought low by failure, poverty, and alcoholism, Esteban hanged himself in a rundown hotel in Tacubaya. Sometimes they show his old movies on television, and I feel like I'm watching a ghost.

At the time, the upside for me was that I got my own room. Till then I'd shared a room with Estelita, my little sister. But when they dubbed me a pervert, my mother thought Estelita might be in danger. They moved her in with the older girls—much to the dismay of Isabel, who was studying at college prep, and Rosa María, who had just graduated as an English-Spanish bilingual secretary.

Héctor wanted to share my room with me. My parents refused. As a consequence of his most recent run-ins with the police and his latest attempts to rape a maid, Héctor slept in the basement under lock and key. They gave him only a few blankets and an old mattress. My father used Hector's former bedroom to store the factory's secret accounts and repeat each lesson from his English records a thousand times: At what time did you go to bed last night, that you are not up yet? I went to bed very late, and I overslept myself. I could not sleep until four o'clock in the morning. My servant did not call me, therefore I did not wake up. I don't know any other adult who actually learned to speak English in less than a year. He had no choice.

I overheard a conversation between my parents. Poor Carlitos. Don't worry, he'll get over it. No, this is going to affect his whole life. What bad luck. How could this have happened to our son? Think of it like an accident, like being hit by a truck. Within a few weeks he won't even remember it. If right now he thinks what we've done is unfair, when he grows up he'll understand that it was for his own good. It's the immorality we imbibe in this country, under the most corrupt regime ever. Look at the magazines, the radio, movies; everything is being done to corrupt the innocent.

In the end, I was alone, nobody could help me. Even Héctor thought it was all a lark, something amusing, a window broken by a stray ball. Neither my father nor my siblings nor Mondragón nor Father Ferrán nor the authors of the tests understood anything. My actions didn't fit the rules they were using to judge me by.

I started going to a new school. I didn't know anybody. Once again I was the foreign intruder. There were neither Jews nor Arabs nor poor kids on scholarship nor battles in the desert, although there was, as always, mandatory English. The first few weeks were hellish. I couldn't stop thinking about Mariana. My parents thought the punishments, the confession, the psychological testing—the results of which I never saw—had cured me. On the sly, however, and to the great dismay of the newspaper vendor, I bought *Vea* and *Vodevil* and abused myself without spilling my seed. The image of Mariana kept reappearing, above and beyond Tongolele, Kalantán, Su Muy Key. No, I wasn't cured; love is a disease in a world where only hatred's natural.

Needless to say, I never saw Jim again. I didn't dare go near our old school or his house.

When I thought about Mariana, the impulse to go see her was mixed with sensations of discomfort and ridicule. How stupid of me, to get into such a mess—it all could have been avoided by simply re-sisting my idiotic urge to declare my love. It was too late for regrets: I did what I had to do, and even now, so many years later, I refuse to deny that I fell in love with Mariana.

XII. *Colonia Roma*

There was a big earthquake in October. A comet blazed by in November. They said these events presaged a nuclear war and the end of the world, or, at the very least, another revolution in Mexico. Then the hardware store, La Sirena, burned down and many people died. By the time the Christmas holidays rolled around, everything had changed for us. My father had sold the factory and been hired as a manager for the North American company that had absorbed his brand of soap. Héctor was studying at the University of Chicago, and my older sisters in Texas.

One day around noon I was on my way home from playing tennis at the Junior Club. I was sitting on a side-facing seat on a bus on the Santa María line reading a Perry Mason novel, when, on the corner of Insurgentes and Álvaro Obregón, Rosales asked the driver for permission and boarded with a box of Adams chewing gum. He saw me. Embarrassed, he jumped quickly off the bus and hid behind a tree near Alfonso y Marcos, where my mother used to go for her permanents and manicures before she had her own car and drove to a salon in Polanco.

Rosales, the poorest boy at my old school, the son of a cleaning lady in a hospital. Everything happened in seconds. I jumped off the bus when it was already in motion, Rosales tried to escape, but I caught up with him. Ridiculous scene: Rosales, please, don't be embarrassed. It's fine that you're working. (I: who had never worked a single day in his life.) Helping your mother is nothing to be ashamed of, on the contrary. (I: playing the role of Dr. Lovesick From Her Soul Hospital.) Come on, look, I'll treat you to an ice cream at La Bella Italia. You can't imagine how glad I am to see you. (I: so magnanimous, with money to spare despite devaluation and inflation.) Rosales: sullen, pale, backing away. Until finally he stopped and looked me in the eyes.

No, Carlitos, I'd rather have a sandwich, if you don't mind. I haven't eaten breakfast. I'm starving. Hey, do you still hold a grudge against me because of our fights? No way, Rosales, those things don't matter anymore. (I: the magnanimous one, able to forgive because I have become invulnerable.) Okay, fine, Carlitos, let's go sit somewhere and talk.

We crossed Obregón, then Insurgentes. So, did

you pass the school year? How did Jim do on his exams? What did they say when I didn't come back? Rosales: silent. We sat down in a sandwich shop. He ordered one chorizo, two beef, and a Sidral Mundet soda. And you, Carlitos, aren't you going to eat? I can't, they're expecting me at home. My mother made my favorite roast beef today. If I eat now, I won't be hungry later. Please bring me a coke, very cold, thanks.

Rosales placed the box of chewing gum on the table. He looked out toward Insurgentes: Packards, Buicks, Hudsons, yellow streetcars, metal lampposts, colorful buses, pedestrians still wearing hats — a scene and a moment that will never be repeated. On the building across the street: General Electric, Calentadores Helvex, Estufas Mabe. A long silence, mutual discomfort. Rosales: very nervous, avoiding my eyes, rubbing his sweaty hands on his worn-out blue jeans.

They brought the order. Rosales took a bite of the chorizo sandwich. Before chewing he took a sip of Sidral to wet it down. It made me sick. Drawn-out hunger and anxiety; he gobbled it down. With his mouth full he asked: And you? Did you pass in spite of changing schools? Are you going somewhere for vacation? On the jukebox "La Múcura" ended and "Riders in the Sky" began. We're going to New York to meet my brothers and sisters for Christmas. We've got reservations at the Plaza. Do you know what the Plaza is? But why don't you answer my questions?

Rosales swallowed saliva, sandwich, and soda. I thought he was going to choke. Well, Carlitos, it's just that, look, I don't know how to say this. The whole class knew everything. What's everything? About his mother. Jim told every single one of us. *He hates you.* We thought what you did was really funny. What a nut job. To top it off, someone saw you confessing in church after your declaration of love. And somehow word got out that they'd taken you to a shrink.

I didn't answer. Rosales kept eating in silence. Then he lifted his eyes and looked at me: I didn't want to tell you, Carlitos, but that's not the worst of it. Naw, someone else should tell you. Just let me finish my sandwiches. They're delicious. I haven't eaten for a whole day. My mother was fired because she tried to organize a union at the hospital. And the guy who lives with her now says that since I'm not his son, he has no obligation to support me. Rosales, I'm really sorry, but it's not my problem, and I've got no reason to get involved. Eat as much as you want and whatever you want—it's on me—but tell me the worst.

Okay, Carlitos, but I'm really sorry, believe me.

Come on, out with it, don't mess with me, Rosales. Spit it out, tell me what you were going to say. It's just that, look, Carlitos, I don't know how to say it. Jim's mother's dead.

Dead? What do you mean, dead? Yeah, dead. Jim's not at school anymore. He's been living in San Francisco since October. His real father came and got him. It was horrible. You have no idea. It seems like she had some kind of fight or something with that Señor, the one Jim said was his father but wasn't. He and his mother—her name was Mariana, right?—were in a cabaret or a restaurant or at a very elegant party in Las Lomas. They were arguing about something she'd said about the thieves in the government, about how they were squandering all the money they stole from the poor. The Señor didn't like her raising her voice in front of his super powerful friends—ministers, foreign millionaires, high-powered money-laundering partners, and all the rest. And he slapped her right there in front of everybody, and he shouted at her that she had no right to talk about honor because she was a whore.

Mariana got up and went home in a taxi and took a bottle of Nembutal or slit her wrists with a razor blade or shot herself or did all of that together, I don't know exactly what she did. Anyway, when Jim woke up he found her dead, in a pool of blood.

He almost died, too, of pain and fear. And since the doorman wasn't there, Jim went to tell Mondragón. He didn't have anybody else. And that was that, the entire school found out. You should have seen the crowd of onlookers and the Green Cross and the official from the public prosecutor's office and the police.

I didn't dare look at her dead, but when they brought her out on the stretcher the sheets were covered in blood. For all of us, it was the worst thing that had ever happened. Jim's mother left him a letter in English, a long letter asking him to forgive her and explaining to him everything I just told you. I think she also left some other notes—maybe even one for you, who knows—but they vanished because the Señor immediately covered up the whole thing, and they forbade us from talking about it among ourselves and especially at home. But you know how rumors spread and how difficult it is to keep a secret. Poor Jim, poor buddy, how much we used to tease him at school. I really regret it.

No way, Rosales. You've got to be pulling my leg. You made up everything you just told me. You saw it in one of those fucking Mexican movies you like so much. You heard it on some crappy XEW soap opera. Those things can't happen. Don't fuck with me like that, please.

It's true, Carlitos. I swear to god it's true. May my mother drop dead if anything I said was a lie. Ask anybody at school. Go talk to Mondragón. Everybody knows about it even though it didn't come out in the papers. I'm surprised you haven't heard anything till now. Remember, I didn't want to be the one to tell you, that's why I hid, not because of the chewing gum. Carlitos, don't look at me like that. Are you crying? I know, it's terrible and hideous what happened. I was in shock, too, like you can't believe. But you're not going to tell me, seriously, at your age, that you were in love with Jim's mother.

Instead of answering I stood up, paid with a ten-peso bill, and, without waiting for the change and without saying goodbye, walked out. I saw death everywhere: in the pieces of animal about to become sandwiches and tacos along with the onions, tomatoes, lettuce, cheese, crema, beans, guacamole, jalapeños. Living animals, like the trees they'd just chopped down on Insurgentes. I saw death in the sodas: Mission Orange, Spur, Ferroquina. In the cigarettes: Belmont, Gratos, Elegantes, Casinos.

I ran down Tabasco, telling myself, trying to tell myself: Rosales is fucking with me, it's a stupid joke, he's always been an asshole. He wanted revenge because I saw him down and out with his box of chewing gum and me with my tennis whites, my Perry

Mason in English, my reservations at the Plaza, and my tennis racket. I don't care if Jim opens the door. I don't care if I make a fool of myself. Even if everyone laughs at me, I want to see Mariana. I'll prove that Mariana's not dead.

I reached the building, dried my tears with a tissue, walked up the stairs, rang the bell to apartment four. A girl about fifteen opened the door. Mariana? No, nobody by the name of Mariana lives here. This is the home of the Morales family. We moved in two months ago. I don't know who might have lived here before us. You should ask the doorman.

While the girl was talking, I could see into a different living room—dirty, poor, disorderly. Without the portrait of Mariana by Semo or the picture of Jim at the Golden Gate Bridge or the images of the Señor "serving his country" with the president's team. Instead of all that: The Last Supper in metallic relief and a tinned wall calendar with images of La Leyenda de los Volcanes.

The doorman was also new in the building. It wasn't Don Sindulfo, the one from before, the old former Zapatista colonel who'd become Jim's friend and sometimes told us stories from the Revolution and cleaned Jim's house because Mariana didn't like having a maid. No, son. I don't know any Don Sindulfo or this Jim you're talking about. There's no Señora Mariana. Don't bug me, kid, just forget it. I offered him twenty pesos. Not if you give me a thousand. I can't take it—I don't know nothing about nothing.

He did, however, take the money and let me carry on my search. At that moment I thought I remembered that the building belonged to the Señor and that he hired Don Sindulfo because his father—the person Jim referred to as "mi abuelito"—had been friends with the old man when they both fought in the Revolution. I rang all the doorbells. I was so ridiculous in my tennis whites, with my racket and my Perry Mason, asking questions, peeking inside, again on the verge of tears. The aroma of sopa de arroz, the aroma of chile rellenos. In all the apartments, they listened to me almost fearfully. How incongruent my tennis whites were. This was the house of death, not a tennis court.

Nope. I've been in this building since 1939 and, as far as I know, no, Señora Mariana has ever lived here. Jim? Don't know him, either. In apartment eight there's a kid about your age, but his name is Everardo. In apartment four? No, an old couple without children used to live there. But I came over here to Jim and Mariana's house a million times. You're imagining things, son. Must be a different street, a different building. Well, off you go; don't waste any more of my time. And don't stick your nose into things that are none of your business—don't stir up trouble. Enough already, son, please. I have to get lunch ready; my husband gets home at two thirty. But, Señora ... go away, son, or I'll call the police, and they'll take you straight to juvenile court.

I went home, and I can't remember what I did next. I must have cried for days. Then we went to New York. I stayed and went to school in Virginia, I remember—I don't even remember the year. Only these flurries, these flickers that bring back everything and the exact words. Only that song that I will never hear again:

> However high the heavens or the skies,
> however deep the ocean lies.

So ancient, so remote, such an impossible story. But Mariana existed, Jim existed, everything existed that I've repeated to myself after such a long time of refusing to confront it. I'll never know if the suicide was true. I never again saw Rosales or anybody else from that era. They demolished the school, they demolished Mariana's building, they demolished my house, and they demolished Colonia Roma. That city ended. That country is finished. There is no memory

of the Mexico of those years. And nobody cares—
who could feel nostalgia for that horror? Everything
came to an end the way the songs on the jukebox
come to an end. I'll never know if Mariana is still
alive. If she were alive today, she'd be eighty years
old.

*

The Magic of Simplicity

For decades, *Battles in the Desert* has been one of the most widely read novels in Mexico. Since its original 1980 serialization in the weekend cultural supplement *Sábado* and its subsequent publication, a year later, by the iconic publisher Ediciones Era, this story of impossible love between a boy and his best friend's mother has established itself as one of the most important novellas in Mexican literature, which boasts such gems in this genre as *Aura* by Carlos Fuentes, *The Hole* by José Revueltas, and *Elsinore: un cuaderno* (Elsinore: a notebook) by Salvador Elizondo, to name just a few.

The considerable reach of this novella is in large part thanks to its readers' word-of-mouth recommendations over the years and the fact that, since its second edition, it became part of standard middle school and high school curricula throughout the country, especially in the capital, Mexico City, awakening among students of successive generations the kind of interest and awe that very few "required" or "compulsory" texts ever generate among adolescents. Cementing the widespread love for *Battles in the Desert* isn't only its detailed portrait of bygone days, its appealing brevity and intimate, confessional tone, but also its glowing emotional credibility, so strong that many readers believe the story to be autobiographical, to the amusement and astonishment of its author.

Born in Mexico City in 1939, just a few months before the start of World War II, José Emilio Pacheco is first introduced to the magic of fiction at the age of eight, during a school trip to the theatre at the Palacio de Bellas Artes to see Salvador Novo's stage adaptation of *Don Quixote*. "On that now distant morning," Pacheco would relate in his 2009 speech accepting the Cervantes Prize, the highest award in the Spanish language, "I discover that there is another reality called fiction. It becomes clear to me that my everyday speech, the language into which I was born and which is my only wealth, can—for those of us able to use it—resemble the music of that show, the colors of the costumes and the houses that lit up the stage." This early calling led him to write what he called "little pirate novels" inspired by the adventure stories—by Salgari, Verne, Dumas—he began to devour around that time, and by his nineteenth birthday he had already tried his hand at every literary genre, publishing his work in newspapers and student magazines. After abandoning his law degree at the National Autonomous University of Mexico to fully devote himself to literature, he became part of the so-called Generación de Medio Siglo (Mexico's midcentury literary generation) along with his friends Sergio Pitol and Carlos Monsiváis, as well as other writers who would rejuvenate Mexico's national literature, such as Salvador Elizondo, Juan Vicente Melo, Juan García Ponce and Inés Arredondo.

The Pacheco, Monsiváis, Pitol triumvirate in particular took pains to marry high and low culture in their works, catching the attention of younger readers. From his poems to his novels, his short stories to his journalism, from his translations, essays and literary criticism, to his historical works, José Emilio Pacheco took a rigorous approach to form and cultivated extreme clarity of content. For forty years, and across several publications, he published his renowned column "Inventario" (Inventory), combining his own special mix of forms (criticism, journalism and the essay) and sharing with the general public his favorite book discoveries as well as his encyclopedic knowledge—all expressed in his unique conversational style, at once erudite and personal. It's beyond question that his writing influenced his readers' tastes and broke ground for many Mexican authors' literary experiments.

Reading *Battles in the Desert*, the reader will note the special magic of Pacheco's writing—that simplicity, so deceptive and so masterful. The narrative voice is a well calibrated device gliding through the reality of things, stories and emotions, always giving the impression that memory never betrays. "Pacheco's craft and mastery make writing look easy," writes Luis Jorge Boone in "José Emilio Pacheco: Un lector fuera del tiempo" (José Emilio Pacheco: a reader outside of time), an essay on the author's work. "Achieving that almost magical ease took Pacheco years of rewrites, edits, cuts. The layers upon layers of work the author put into his books over the years is legendary."

Lengthy prose poems he stripped down in their final versions to pithy lines. Translations took years of painstaking transference—his translation of Eliot's *Four Quartets* into Spanish, for example, consumed more than two decades. Works of prose fiction went on being refined until the very last day their author was able to revise them: they were edited again and again in a firm rejection of conclusiveness. "I do not accept the idea of a definitive text," Pacheco wrote in his notes to his complete poems, *Tarde o temprano: Poemas 1958–2009* (Sooner or later:

poems 1958–2009). "For as long as I am alive, I will go on editing myself."

For its thirtieth anniversary edition, he went so far as to amend several sections in *Battles in the Desert*, including its ending, even changing the age of Mariana (a character inspired by the actress Rita Hayworth, according to Pacheco) to imply that the story was being narrated in more recent times: "I will never know if Mariana is still alive. If she is, she would be eighty years old," declares the narrator of that anniversary edition. The first serial *Sábado* version was shorter, and Pacheco said that Fernando Benítez, the editor, had had to practically snatch it out of his hands to prevent him making further revisions.

That original version arrived, essentially complete, in a feverish session at his typewriter the day after the opening of an exhibition of lithographs by Vicente Rojo, where Pacheco had been interviewed about the poems he'd written to accompany Rojo's works, channeling the horrors the artist had witnessed as a child in Barcelona during the Civil War. During that interview, and on subsequent occasions when he was asked about the origin of *Battles in the Desert*, Pacheco mentioned an idea that had recently affected him (and which he attributed to the writer Graham Greene): that childhood love, being hopeless, is also the saddest. The next day, from that one idea emerged the entire story of young Carlos' woes—this was the story that Pacheco would continue to work on, revising it again and again until its 1981 publication by Era, at that time led by Neus Espresate, the legendary publisher who managed to persuade Pacheco that *Battles in the Desert* was a novella, and that it should be published separately and not as part of a collected stories, as Pacheco was convinced it should be.

During an interview shortly before his death in 2014, Pacheco was asked why nostalgia so imbues his stories. "We can only write about what is no more," he replied. "Writing is an attempt to preserve something in the midst of all that disappears and is destroyed each day. But there is no nostalgia in my texts: there is memory."

And indeed, there is no nostalgia for former times in *Battles in the Desert*; in its place there is testimony, recovery, and even denunciation of the historical transformations that, from the 1940s onwards, would alter the colonial features of Mexico City and see it transformed into a megalopolis of skyscrapers and traffic that eventually engulfed the entire Anahuac valley, or Valley of Mexico, making room for the millions of migrants who would descend upon the capital looking for better living conditions: peasants displaced by the new agricultural systems, professionals fed up with the sleepy provinces, and foreigners fleeing fascism. And although leaders would continue to hail the ideals of the Mexican Revolution—land for the dispossessed, decent wages for the proletariat and State intervention in economic affairs—a growing alliance between politicians and businessmen would usher in an era of unbalanced growth and social inequality. The consumerism of the opulent classes would exist hand in hand with the social neglect of the undermined majority, and the corruption that oils the wheels of commerce and industry would become commonplace. Though a large part of the capital's population would preserve their traditional, provincial customs around food, family and religion, the younger generations enthusiastically embraced the "North Americanization" made inevitable by the introduction of brands, food, technology, fashion, music genres, TV series and movies from the USA. This schism is precisely the "pivotal moment" that Pacheco so lucidly incarnates in his narrator's intimate, familiar voice, telling us about the world of his childhood, the joys and sorrows of his school and family life, and that first passion, which hits him like a stab wound out of nowhere.

The story of an impossible love, the tale of desire in its purest and most defenseless form, the portrait

of a city and country at the dawn of a radical trans-
formation, the critical, unsparing evocation of a society plagued by institutional corruption (still the
scourge of modern Mexico), *Battles in the Desert* is a
reckoning with the past and an attempt to preserve
what was, what is no more—that love and horror
which Pacheco shows us with moving simplicity.

FERNANDA MELCHOR, 2021